Give Up, Gecko!

A Folktale from Uganda

retold by
Margaret Read MacDonald

illustrated by
Deborah Melmon

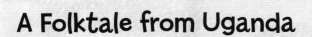

Amazon Children's Publishing

Days and days, waiting for rain.
     The animals needed to drink.
"Let's dig for water," said the animals.
"The one who finds water can be our chief."
 All the animals wanted to be chief.
"Let's use our tusks!" bellowed Elephant.
"Tusks! Tusks!" shouted Boar.

"No! Let's use our horns!" hollered Rhino.

"Horns! Horns!" agreed Deer.

Some animals didn't have horns.

Some animals didn't have tusks.

"Let's STOMP!" said Hippo.

"Everybody has feet!"

"Not me," whispered Snake.

But the animals were already voting.

"STOMP! STOMP! We will STOMP!"

"Me first!" Elephant found a
good place to dig and began.
"Elephant! Elephant!
Heavy! Heavy! Heavy!
Elephant! Elephant!
STOMP! STOMP! STOMP!"

It was hot. Elephant got tired.
"Elephant! Elephant!
Heavy! Heavy! Heavy!
Elephant! Elephant!
Stomp! Stomp! Stomp!
No water here. I give up."

"My turn!" shouted Hippo.
"Hippo! Hippo!
 Heavy! Heavy! Heavy!
 Hippo! Hippo!
 STOMP! STOMP! STOMP!"

Hippo churned up the dust.

The hole got deeper and deeper.

Then Hippo got tired.

"No water here. I give up."

"Rhino! Rhino!
Heavy! Heavy! Heavy!
Rhino! Rhino!
STOMP! STOMP! STOMP!

I give up."

Buffalo. . . Giraffe. . . .

All the big animals took a turn.

All the big animals. . . gave up.

So the middle-sized animals tried.

Warthog. . . Hyena. . . .

Monkey thought he could do it.

"Monkey! Monkey!

Heavy! Heavy! Heavy!

Monkey! Monkey! BANANAS!

Bye-bye!"

Soon the middle-sized animals all. . . gave up.

Now the *little* animals wanted to try.

The big animals were laughing.

"Ha! What can *they* do?"

The big animals were right.

The little animals didn't have any luck either.

Iguana tried. . . . Rabbit tried. . . .

"Rabbit! Rabbit!

Heavy! Heavy! Heavy!"

Rabbit had no patience.

"What can a *rabbit* do? I give up!"

"Nobody can do it," said Elephant.

"Nobody found water. Let's go home."

Then they heard a tiny voice.

"*I* didn't get a turn yet.

Let *me* try."

The animals looked all around.

Where was that tiny voice coming from?

It was *Gecko!*

"I can do it! Let me try!"

The animals all started laughing.

What could a silly little animal like Gecko do? Nothing!

"Let's go home," said Elephant. "There is no water here."

But Gecko had jumped into
the deep, deep hole.
"Gecko! Gecko!
Heavy! Heavy! Heavy!
Gecko! Gecko!
Stomp! Stomp! Stomp!"

"Look at that silly little gecko!
He thinks he is *heavy*! GIVE UP, GECKO!"

Gecko was so embarrassed.
He turned bright pink all over.
"Gecko is turning pink!" Hippo
laughed. "Give up, Gecko!"

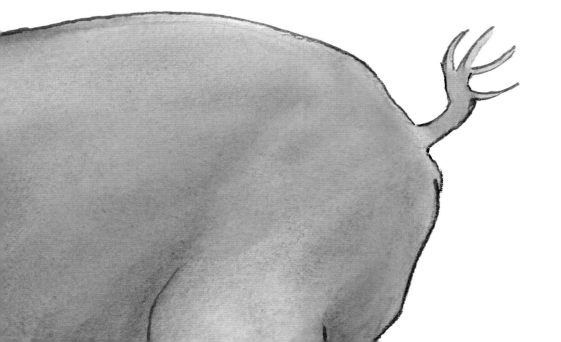

"They can laugh.
I won't give up!"
"Gecko! Gecko!
Heavy! Heavy! Heavy!
Gecko! Gecko!
Stomp! Stomp! Stomp!"

He stomped for one hour.
"Gecko! Gecko!

Heavy!

Heavy!

Heavy!

Gecko!

Gecko!

Stomp!

Stomp!

Stomp!"

All of the animals shouted,

"GIVE UP, GECKO!"

"Gecko! Gecko! . . ." Two hours.
"GIVE UP, GECKO!"
"Gecko! Gecko! . . ." Three hours.
"GIVE UP, GECKO!"
The sun was about to go down
and Gecko was still stomping.

Suddenly . . .

"My toes are wet! My toes are wet!"

Gecko was stomping in WATER!

"Gecko! Gecko! Heavy! Heavy! Heavy!

Gecko! Gecko! SPLASH! SPLASH! SPLASH!"

"Out of the WAY!"
Elephant THREW Gecko out of the
hole and he began to stomp.
"Elephant! Elephant!
Heavy! Heavy! Heavy!
Elephant! Elephant!
STOMP! STOMP! STOMP!
I'm the new chief!"
hollered Elephant!
"I found the water!"

But all the animals saw what had happened.
"Get that Elephant out of there!" they shouted.
"Elephant didn't find the water. Gecko did!"

So Gecko jumped back down in the hole again.

All the animals started shouting,

"Gecko! Gecko!

Heavy! Heavy! Heavy!

Gecko! Gecko!

DON'T GIVE UP!"

Slowly the water began to rise.

It came up to his little knees. . . .

It came up to his little waist. . . .

It came up to his little neck. . . .

"WATER!"

The water was spraying all over! Everybody
was dancing and singing.

"Gecko! Gecko! He found the water!
Gecko! Gecko! He's the ONE!"

The animals built a special house for Gecko, right by
the side of the water.

"You all helped dig," said Gecko. "Everybody can share."

"Yes, we all helped dig," said the animals. "But you,
Gecko, you were the one who never gave up!"

This tale was inspired by "Chameleon and Elephant" in Okot p'Bitek's **Hare and Hornbill** (London: Heinemann, 1978). The tales of p'Bitek were drawn from Ugandan Lango and Acoli sources. For a discussion of the tale, see **The Storyteller's Start-up-Book: Finding, Learning, Performing, and Using Folktales** by Margaret Read MacDonald (August House, 1993), pp. 145-146. Stories of animals digging for water are found in many cultures. In **The Storyteller's Sourcebook: A Subject, Title, and Motif-Index to Folklore Collections for Children 1983-1999** by Margaret Read MacDonald and Brian Sturm (Gale Research, 2000), you can find versions of Motif A2233.1 **Animals refuse to dig well** from Ghana, Liberia, Bantu, Ewe, Australia Aborigine, China, Venezuela, Cherokee, and African-American sources.

—M.R.M.

For Jennifer Whitman's Grade 2 class at Bonn International School,
with thanks for helping shape this tale just the way you like it. –M.R.M.

For my sister, Patti —D.M.

Text copyright © 2013 by Margaret Read MacDonald
Illustrations copyright © 2013 by Deborah Melmon

Amazon Publishing
Attn: Amazon Children's Publishing
P.O. Box 400818
Las Vegas, NV 89149
www.amazon.com/amazonchildrenspublishing

Library of Congress Cataloging-in-Publication Data available upon request.
ISBN 9781477816356 (hardcover)   9781477866351 (ebook)

The illustrations are rendered in watercolor and colored pencil and manipulated in Photoshop.
Book design by Vera Soki
Editor: Margery Cuyler

Printed in China (R)
First edition
10 9 8 7 6 5 4 3 2 1